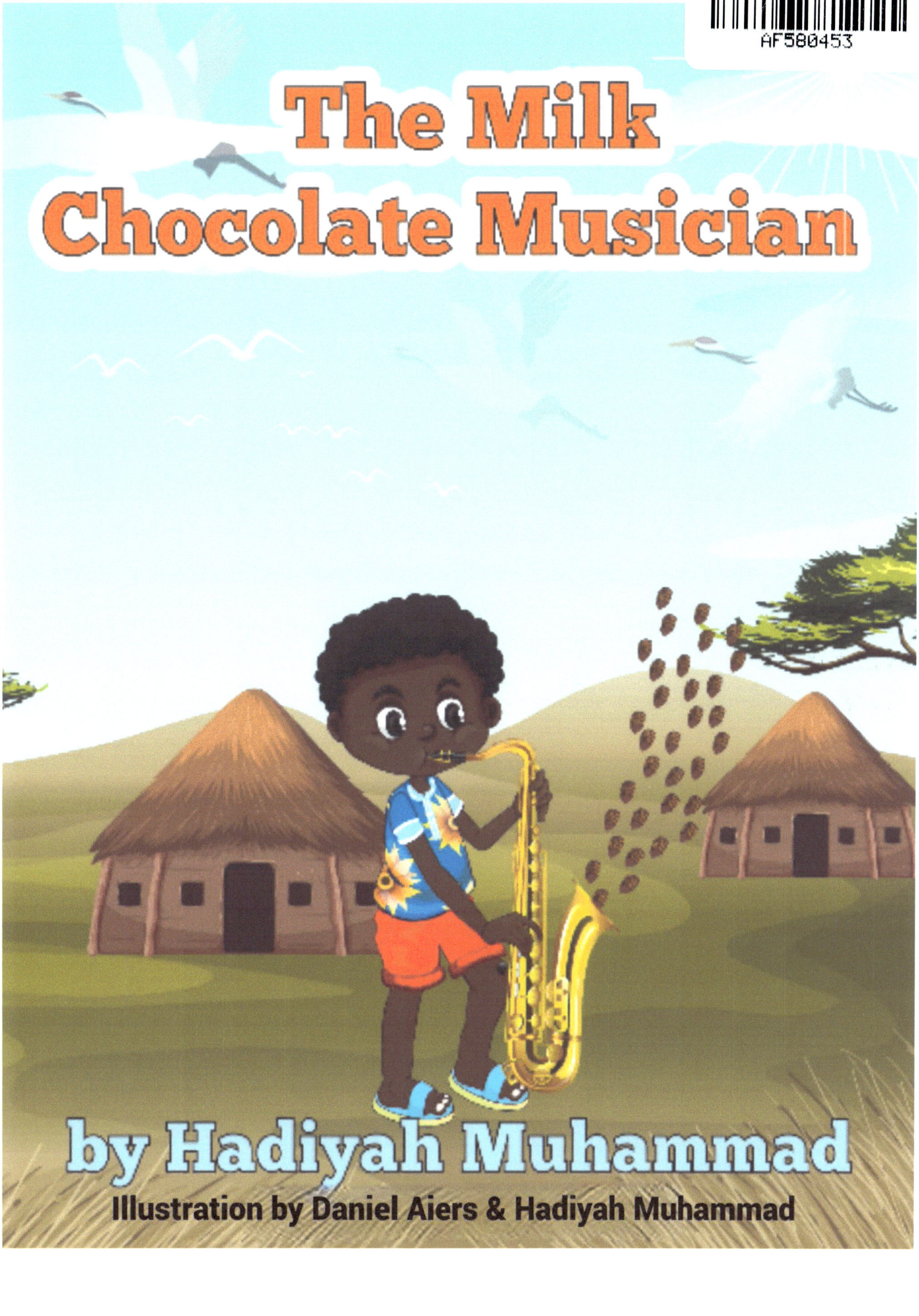

The Milk Chocolate Musician

by Hadiyah Muhammad

Illustration by Daniel Aiers & Hadiyah Muhammad

the Milk Chocolate Musician

by Hadiyah Muhammad

Illustration by Daniel Aiers & Hadiyah Muhammad

the Milk Chocolate Musician

Cover and Interior Design by Daniel Aiers
& Hadiyah Muhammad

ISBN-9798363946295

For more information, email
hadiyahnm@gmail.com

Dedication

To all beautiful melanated children

Once there was a young, flashy musician named Bubba Kente who loved milk chocolate. He and his shiny, gold saxophone, Charlie, lived in a small hut on Buttercup Island.

"Peace and Blessings, Charlie!" Said Bubba, stretching his arms. I'm in the mood to create music magic today; how about you? I want to share our special art form with the village people.

Bubba and Charlie were admired from near and far for their unique Afrikan rhythm, Kutijahgah. This style revolutionized simple notes into chocolate musical masterpieces.

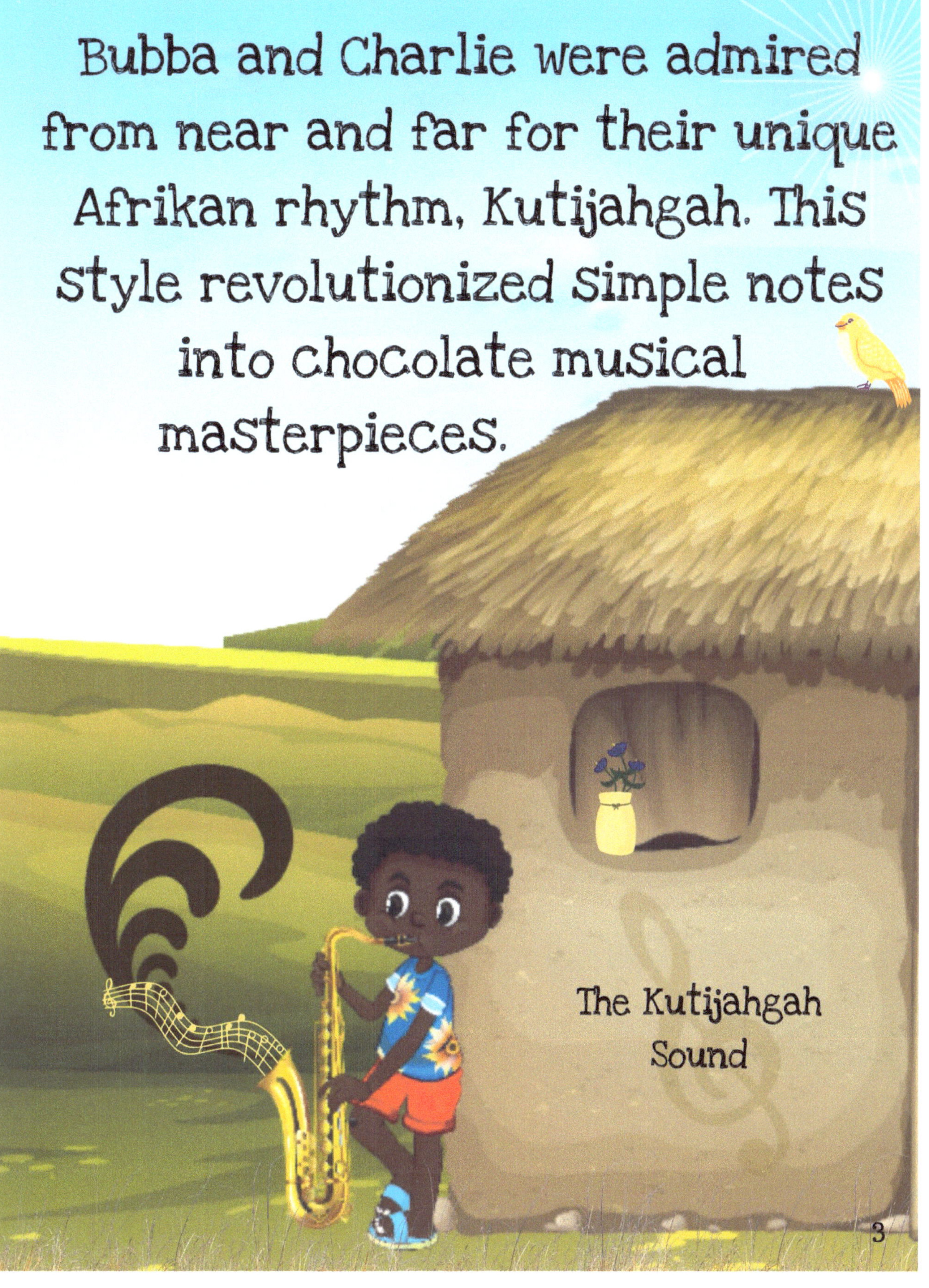

So, one hot and sunny afternoon, Bubba and Charlie began to bebop down Cocoa Cluster Road to the nearby village, Crunch Delight Lane, to play some smashing chocolate tunes for the children.

"Here he comes! Here he comes!" yelled one of the village children as he darted out the door with a lollipop. "Whew, listen to that lovely umpta gumpta sound," uttered Mama Asiyah, a beloved elder.

Bubba and Charlie ignited the village people with their magnificent performance. A bazillion milk chocolate candies burst from the bottom of the carved woodwind instrument. There were chocolate candies everywhere.

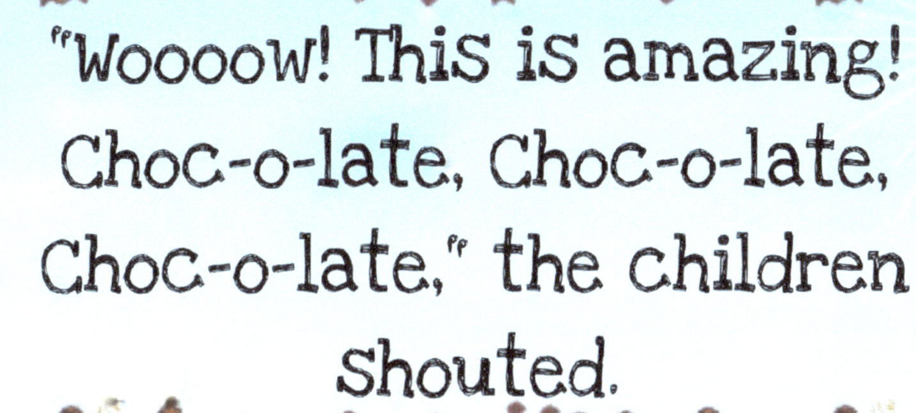

"Woooow! This is amazing! Choc-o-late, Choc-o-late, Choc-o-late," the children shouted.

"You can eat as much as you want. The choc-o-late never ends," mumbled Bubba, with a mouth full of crispy crunch.

Guess what? The children ate as much as they wanted. They ate so much candy that day chocolate wrappers covered the sandy roads.

"What have you done?" Spewed the angry woman wearing red lipstick. "Just look at all those children; they're going to be..."

"Wait! please, listen. I only wanted to make the village happy with our Kutijahgah music and chocolate bonanza.

"You call this happy? Look what you've done to our village," the mean old man hollered with a rake in his hand. "Take your milk chocolate music and your trash playing saxophone with you."

Bubba was sad as the harsh words pierced his soul. He ate a piece of the chocolate goop off Charlie. And suddenly, Mama Asiyah turned to Bubba Kente and said, "young warrior your music is magical. You are the milk chocolate musician who brought joy to the village."

Let your heart be light and happy, so

you can play us more Kutijahrah tunes." So, Bubba played his heart out. Bubba Kente and his magical sax, Charlie skipped down Mingus Drop Road playing a new song and stirring up more chocolate tunes from the milk chocolate musician.

Do the Knowledge

1 piece of chocolate

C ___ ___ ___ ___

Name the color of each candy

____

____

____

How many chocolate squares

Total # ___________

What is the name of the fruit on top of the shake? ___________

What is the color of the fruit on top of the shake? ___________

Answer key: cake; gold, fushia, turquoise blue; 18; cherry; red

Do the Knowledge

This chart is not only for learning about kente colors and meanings, but as a literacy tool to teach colors, pronounce words, count words, and embrace the beauty of yourself and your culture. We must teach our little one(s) early.

COLOR	MEANING	Name/Repeat
Blue	PEACE, TOGETHERNESS; LOVE & HARMONY	○ ○
Black	MATURITY, SPIRITUAL ENERGY, MOURNING, FUNERAL & PASSING RITES	○ ○
Gold	HIGH WORTH, RICHNESS, FERTILITY, ROYALTY, PROSPERITY, WEALTH	○ ○
Green	LAND, CROPS, VEGETATION, HARVEST, GROWTH, SPIRITUAL GROWTH & RENEWAL	○ ○
Yellow	HIGH WORTH, RICHNESS, FERTILITY, ROYALTY, PROSPERITY, WEALTH	○ ○
Gray	HEALING RITUALS, CLEANSING RITUALS, SYMBOLIZES ASH	○ ○
Pink	FEMININE, MILDNESS & FEMININE QUALITIES	○ ○
	PURENESS, CLEANSING RITES & FESTIVALS	○ ○
Maroon	MOTHER EARTH & HEALING	○ ○
Red	DEATH, FUNERALS & MOURNING	○ ○
Purple	FEMININE, WOMANHOOD, WORN BY GIRLS	○ ○
Silver	PEACE & JOY, REFERENCING TO THE MOON	○ ○

Color Chart and Meanings retrieved from Crystalkente.com

Do the Knowledge

Story fun facts

1. What is the name of the main character?

____

2. What is the name of the Afrikan rhythmic sound in the story?

____

3. What is the name of the saxophone?

____

4. What came out of the saxophone when it was played?

____

Answer key: Bubba Kente; The Kutijahgah Sound; Charlie; milk chocolate candies

5. Name three villages in the book with chocolate names

____

6. Match the characters with their proper description

Mama Asiyah	"Look what you've done to our village"
Charlie	Flashy musician/young warrior
Children	Beloved elder
Angry Woman	Live in the village Crunch Delight Lane
Mean old man	Gold saxophone
Bubba Kente	Wearing red lipstick

7. Unscramble the words

kobo ______________________________

lackb ______________________________

lkim ______________________________

ocoatelch ______________________________

usciianm ______________________________

Answer Key: Buttercup Island, Cocoa Cluster Lane, Crunch Delight Lane; a. book; b. black; c. milk; d. chocolate; e. musician

8. Name the picture and color

9. Name five milk chocolate candies

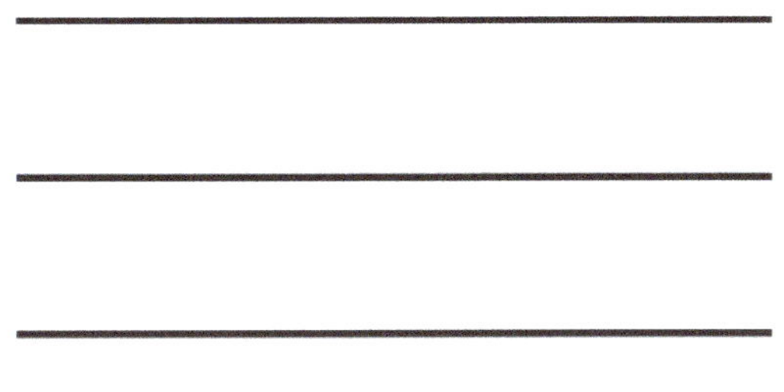

10. Name the different insects and animals you find in the story

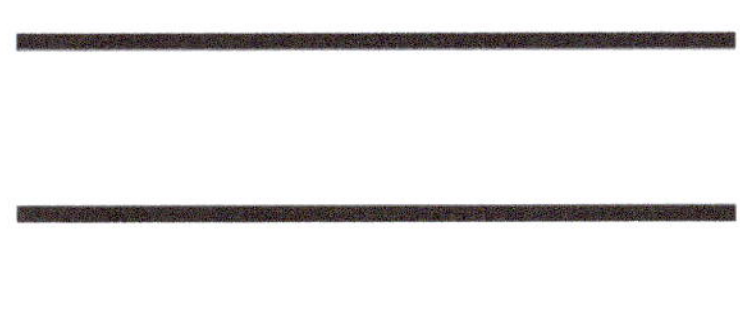

Answer key: birds; elephants; ducks; bees; flies; butterflies

Dear parents/readers, young readers, and non-readers,

Thank you for joining us on this literary journey with The Milk Chocolate Musician. Some of the activities may appear to be advanced for non-readers or young readers; however, these activities are guided practices for an advanced reader or adult to read to or do with their little one(s.)

With gratitude,

Hadiyah Muhammad

The milk chocolate musician is a fun, enlightening, and cultural story to spark the imagination and creativity of young minds.

www.ingramcontent.com/pod-product-compliance
Lightning Source LLC
LaVergne TN
LVHW071136160826
845679LV00005B/1307
* 9 7 9 8 3 6 3 9 4 6 2 9 5 *